Dear Santa

AMY LAURENS

OTHER WORKS

SANCTUARY SERIES

Where Shadows Rise
Through Roads Between
When Worlds Collide

KADITEOS SERIES

How Not To Acquire A Castle
How Not To Ring The Hero's Bell
How Not To Take Over The World

SHORT STORY COLLECTIONS

Of Sea Foam and Blood
Darkness and Good

NON-FICTION

How To Write Dogs
How To Theme
How To Create Cultures
How To Create Life
How To Map
The 32 Worst Mistakes People Make About
Dogs

Find other works by the author at
www.amylaurens.com

Dear Santa

INKLET #23

AMY LAURENS

www.inkprintpress.com

Print ISBN: 978-1-925825-23-7
eBook ISBN: 9781386014393

www.inkprintpress.com

National Library of Australia Cataloguing-in-Publication Data
Laurens, Amy 1985 –
Dear Santa
40 p.
ISBN: 978-1-925825-23-7
Inkprint Press, Canberra, Australia
1. Fiction—Horror 2. Fiction—Short Stories

First Print Edition: December 2019
Cover design © Inkprint Press
Interior art © Thea van Diepen

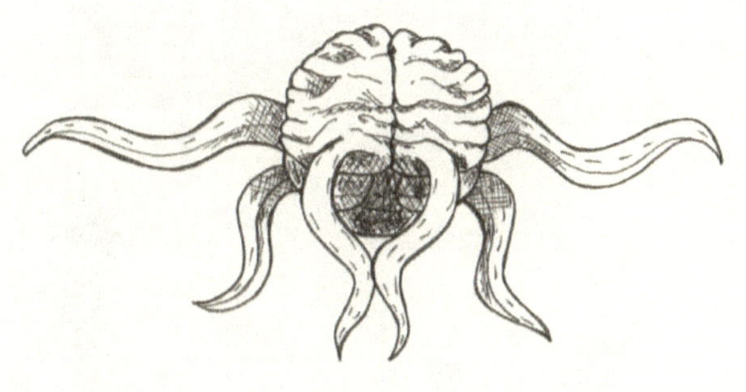

DEAR SANTA

Dear SAntA,
for christmas i wish everyone else in my family had more brains. i'm really sick of my sister being so stupid. And mum and Dad are so mean sometimes.
yours,
Tommy.

PS i'm NOT little. if any one calls me LITTLE Tommy again you might not be able to bring me any presents. sorry. TB.

Tommy stared down at the sheet of paper with his tongue between his teeth and his brow wrinkled. That looked about right.

He folded it up, tucked it into the envelope, and sealed it. He pulled a face. Envelopes tasted ick.

Tommy bounced down the stairs to the kitchen and tugged on his mum's sleeve. "Mum, Mum!"

"Tommy, why aren't you in bed?" she said, without turning around.

"Mum, I need you to post this letter! You have to post it quick, it's nearly Christmas and it has to get to Santa in time!" He waved the letter up at her.

She smiled and took it from him. "I'll post it when I go to get your sister from Betty's, okay?"

Tommy bounced on his toes. "Will it get there in time?"

She tousled his hair. "I think so."

Tommy ran back to his room and

flopped on his bed. He stared at the ceiling. Mum said she'd post the letter, but what if she forgot? What if she only *said* she would? It was Christmas tomorrow. There wasn't much time.

He tossed and turned and eventually fell asleep.

Tommy blinked himself awake. He stared at his door for a minute, feeling dozy. Then he bolted upright. "It's Christmas!"

He leapt out of bed, whipped on his bathrobe, and pounded down the hall. He bashed on Samantha's door as he passed, grinning as he heard her yell. He took the stairs three at a time and bounded into the living room.

Presents!

He pranced around the Christmas tree, snatching at the brightly wrapped gifts. The blue one was his, the one with the huge gold ribbon too, and the bike in the corner. "Come on!" he yelled. "Faster!"

His mother stumbled into the room, rubbing the sleep from her eyes.

His father yawned and stretched before plopping down on the couch. "We're here, kiddo," he said. "Go ahead."

Tommy pouted. "Sam isn't here yet. Do I have to wait for her?"

"She's coming, dear," said Mum. "Just a moment."

"Sam!" Tommy hollered. "Hurry up!"

She stomped into the room, eyes mostly closed, hair teased up like a fluffy halo. She collapsed onto the beanbag and folded her arms across her chest.

"Shut up," she told him. "I'm here."

Tommy jumped for joy. "Presents!" He dove at the stack, pulling them out with both hands and tossing them to his family.

Soon, everyone had a large pile in front of them, and the others had woken up enough to laugh and smile.

"What are these?" Tommy's mother asked, holding up a strangely-shaped package in green, the size of a football.

"I don't know," his father answered, "but I have one too."

"We all do," said Samantha, pointing at hers on the floor.

Tommy pouted. "I don't." He grabbed his sister's and tried rattling it. "What's inside?"

"I don't know," Mother said, frowning. "Who are they from?"

"Open them!" Tommy bounced on the edge of Samantha's beanbag, and she was too excited about her strange parcel to mind.

"On the count of three," Samantha said, sliding one finger under the edge of the wrapping. "One, two..."

"THREE!" Tommy shouted, tearing at her paper.

She batted him away and he sprawled on the ground.

"Look!" She held it up.

It was brownish grey, kind of squidgy. A ball? he wondered. Some sort of cushion?

The rest of the wrapping dropped away and he stared at it.

"It... it looks like a *brain*," Samantha said, mouth twisted in disgust.

"I think it is," said Dad, holding up his.

"Weird." Tommy poked the brain, wondering what it could do. The brain twitched. He gasped, and scrambled towards his parents to see if their brains had moved too.

Samantha screamed.

He whirled around. The brain was pressed against her face, thin tendrils grasping her head as she thrashed against it.

Tommy moved towards her but froze as another scream sounded behind him.

"Mum! Dad!" he shouted.

But they were too busy to notice; the brains sucked squelchily at their faces. Mum shrieked and leapt to her feet. She ran forward, right into the Christmas tree. It toppled over, tangling her in the cord of lights and tinsel.

Dad stood, trying to follow her voice, hands waving in front of him. He bellowed as the brain gave an extra loud slurp, and tripped to the ground.

Tommy shrank back under the lip of the sofa, whimpering.

Samantha screamed again, tearing frantically at the brain. But it was no use; within minutes all three family members slumped motionless on the ground.

The brains slurped happily.

Tommy cried.

THE MAKING OF

Look, I'm sorry, okay? I don't actually know what I was thinking. I apologise for the trauma. Don't open strange Christmas presents.

(Also don't wish horrible things on your family, I guess? Especially when magical and maybe fae things might be listening?)

So, this was definitely in my 'stupidity causes horrific death' era, but beyond that, I don't even know, and I'm not sure I ever did, to be honest. This just… happened.

It was 2009. I was learning to write short stories by participating in sort-of weekly challenges with friends. It seems at least *plausible* that this came from one of those, right? Especially when you consider that one of said friends was the inestimable short horror writer Merc Rustad.

I expect there's a bit of sideways allusion to *Harry Potter* in there, too, what with the flying brains and all. It was right in the middle of the period in my life where I was rereading them every year, after all ☺

So yeah. Sorry for the trauma. Don't open strange presents, be nice to your family, and if you ever get the chance to make a wish, make sure you make it thoughtfully.

DOWNLOAD YOUR FREE EBOOK

When you buy a print book from Inkprint Press, we like to say THANK YOU by offering you the ebook for free!

Please head to www.inkprintpress.com/inklets/23/ and the use the coupon INK23LET to get your copy of this Inklet in epub AND mobi today!
(Coupon will only work once.)

HOW NOT TO ACQUIRE A CASTLE

CHAPTER ONE

ON A HARD PLASTIC CHAIR IN THE FRONT row of the Great Hall in the world's fifth-best evil overlording academy, with its red-wooden parquetry floor that spoke of wealth and the beige, square panels of sound-boards speaking of conservatism on the walls, Mercury sat, pointedly not sweating.

Partly, this was because the Academy Administrators had deigned to turn on the air-conditioning earlier in the day, in recognition of the fact that the hall would be packed out with approximately six hundred bodies, all here to celebrate the graduation of about a third of that crowd.

But mostly, Mercury was pointedly not sweating because she made it a point never to sweat, sweat being an indication that she was working hard, and hard work being antithetical to her way of life.

However. If she *had* been sweating right now, it would not have been due to the uncomfortable warmth of six hundred packed bodies that even the air-conditioning system couldn't completely shift, or, in fact, from overexertion. Instead, it would have been caused by an even more unfamiliar concept in Mercury's emotional vocabulary: nervousness.

Mercury did not *get* nervous. Mercury got things *done*.

So the fact that she was sitting here, in the front row of the Great Hall, about to graduate from Evil Overlording Academy (with distinction), and was feeling *nervous...* She crumpled the black paper program in her pale fists. It made her furious, that's what it did.

Abjectly furious, that snooty-tooty Deviran with his stupid morals and his stupid I-don't-want-to-be-here and his stupid Overlords-are-empty-figureheads and his stupid face sitting ten people over, looking implacable with his deep brown skin and barely-there, precision-groomed beard, as though he knew it gave him a stupid air of alluringly stupid mystery…

Mercury scowled and searched for the train of thought that had been derailed, yet again, by Deviran's stupidity.

Ah. Yes. She was angry because she was nervous because she wasn't abso-lutely entirely one hundred and fifty percent sure that she'd beaten Deviran in their final exams, and 1) being anything less than a hundred and fifty percent certain of anything made her cranky, and 2) being beaten by Deviran for dux of the year would be utterly unbearable. She flicked away a piece of fluff that had become snagged under her immaculately magenta-painted nails and smoothed out the black paper program.

In the front corner of the hall, the starkly-attired string quartet with their traditional black instruments began play-ing the March of the Oncoming Doom. The screechy scrapes of hundreds of chairs on the hall's wooden floor sounded as the crowd climbed to its collective feet.

Mercury sat with her arms firmly folded for a few moments longer, until her best friend Sparky kicked her in the ankle.

"Get up, idiot," Sparky hissed, hints of real flame flickering through her flame-coloured pixie cut.

"No," Mercury said, flouncing to her feet and tossing her own glossy brown hair back over her shoulders. Four years she'd been playing by the Academy's rules in order to get what she wanted, and she'd had just about enough. Other people's rules should only be applied to plebs too stupid to invent their own.

Sparky rolled her eyes somewhere over Mercury's head before focusing on the stage, where the ceremonial party had begun entering.

Mercury clenched her jaw and narrowed her own eyes as the teachers of the Evil Overlording Academy filed onto the stage, dressed in their formal finery. Each teacher had their own distinctive look that matched their personality and their Overlording style, from severe charcoal suits to jet-black leathers, pastel ballgowns and gem-toned lingerie and eye-blinding spandex, and even on one tiny old woman at the back, worn jeans and a grey flannel shirt. She was the one to watch out for, of course; Mercury could respect an Overlord who was confident enough in their abilities that they didn't need to telegraph them. It wasn't a look *she* would consider, of course, but still. She could respect it.

The band's march finished and, after a moderately awkward pause, the crowd sat. The Principal, pale skin and dark hair matching his suspiciously vampiric red-and-black suit, took the podium, and Mercury narrowed her eyes. He was doing a superb job of hiding his emotions—he was a premier Evil Overlord, after all—but she was Mercury, and unlike anyone else, she had the benefit of being able to rummage through people's consciousnesses. She was better at adding things *into* people's minds than taking information out, but he was telegraphing fear loudly enough that she could sense it without trying overly much.

Mercury pursed her lips.

Hmm.

The Principal cleared his throat at the blackened-wood podium, and the fear made it into his usually-unreadable eyes. "Before we begin," he said, and Mercury's stomach did a peculiar kind of flip-flop. "I have a pressing announcement to make regarding the safety of our students and their families."

He cleared his throat again and took out a sheet of paper from his pocket, unfolding it carefully and smoothing out the creases before beginning again. "The Council"—quiet booing echoed around the hall, and Mercury tsked impatiently—"have asked me to recommend that students from Tumul Tuos seriously consider postponing their return to town for a few days. The city is dealing with a *situation* at present which may present a danger to our students' health and safety."

Mercury's hands fisted at her sides and she forced herself to remain seated. What was wrong with her city? What had the Council mucked up now? A risk to the students' safety? There had to be more he wasn't telling them. Gently, Mercury tugged on his consciousness, implanting the suggestion that it might be better to share the news than to keep it secret. After all, how could they fight an enemy they didn't know?

"There are, ah…" He trailed off, glancing side to side as though wondering why his mouth had decided to continue.

Mercury didn't snicker, but she did press her lips together in satisfaction.

The Principal took a deep, steadying breath and seemed to change tack. "There has been one death already. The family have already been notified, so it is with much regret that I must inform you that Woovermyer will no longer be with us at the Evil Overlording Academy."

Murmurs broke out around the room, not all of them sad—to be expected in a school devoted to raising the next generation of dictators (ish) and despots (of sorts).

Mercury, however, crushed her program in her left hand, fist so tight her nails bit her palm.

"You okay?" Sparky murmured.

Mercury gave a single, tense shake of her head and stared at the podium. Dead. Livie Woovermyer was dead in *her city*. And the Council hadn't done anything to stop it. Couldn't do anything to stop it, probably, given they'd warned the students to stay away. Livie hadn't been the strongest candidate in the year level, but she was no lightweight, either. It would take a lot of power to kill a Seven.

Enough was enough. A good thing Mercury was about to graduate at the top of the class, giving her the right to knock the lowest ranking current Overlord off their perch. Tumul Tuos would be hers in a matter of hours. And then there'd be no more of these wasteful deaths. Her city would be safe at last.

Madame Pompadour was up the front now, elbow gloves the same glimmery silver colour as her elaborate, piled-curls wig, eyelids gleaming with matching silver eye shadow, and abruptly Mercury realised Madame was there to make the announcement that would change her life forever. She leaned forward in her seat, ready to stand when her name was called.

"And now the announcement you've all been dying for," the Political Alliances teacher trilled, the frills on her evening gown fluttering as she moved. "The dux of this year's cohort!"

Sweat slicked Mercury's palms. Irritated, she reached over and wiped them on Sparky's thigh.

Sparky pushed Mercury's hands back into her own personal space bubble and Mercury, nervous to the edge of distraction, let her.

"Will you please join me in welcoming to the stage, our wonderful dux for this year, Deviran Goodsmith!"

Mercury froze halfway to standing. "Did she just say Deviran?" she whispered furiously to Sparky.

Sparky hauled her forcibly back down into her seat. "Yes," she hissed back. "Sit down, you're making a fool of yourself."

Mercury's spine snapped upright as she sat, and she arranged the folds of her long black skirt demurely. "No I'm not." She closed her eyes. "Deviran's going up to the stage, isn't he?" Even at a whisper, the misery in her voice was clear, but this time, she didn't care.

Sparky reached over and squeezed her hand.

Mercury squeezed back, lacing her fingers through Sparky's, and held tight as all her plans and dreams vanished in front of her.

A stone had landed in her chest. That must be it.

Or some strange sort of magic that made her chest contract and sink, and made the world distort for just a moment, long enough to trick her into thinking Deviran had beaten her so that someone could jump in front of her and yell SUR-PRISE!

Any moment now.

Any moment.

She refused to open her eyes and watch Deviran parading across the stupid stage like some stupid stupid-person, receiving his stupid medal and stupid symbolic crest pin.

It was that last exam question. She'd known Deviran would pull out his ridiculous 'Evil Overlords are merely figureheads, the Business Guild is where the power really lies' rant that everyone had heard a million times back when he was younger and angrier, and she'd tried to counter it, she really had.

She'd argued for the importance of the Overlording position, for the power of having a symbolic figure to unite the population in their hatred, for having a person able to make all the difficult, necessary decisions the Council was too weak and spineless to make... But it hadn't been enough. Everything she'd worked for, everything she'd set out to prove—and it wasn't enough.

There were words, there were names, and then forever later, once she'd died twice already, Sparky elbowed her in the ribs. "Come on," Sparky muttered. "We're up next."

And sure enough, there was a shuffling of presenters as the last of the Powers Behind The Thone graduates departed the stage, and the next speaker announced in threatening, funereal tones, "The Over-lording cohort."

Mercury blinked furiously and followed Sparky to the end of the line at the right side of the stage. The other candidates proceeded one at a time across the stage, two girls and then stupid Deviran, and then a handful more and then Sparky, and then the speaker was calling her name.

Hands fisted, Mercury tossed her head high, climbed the four steps, and marched across the stage. She wouldn't look at them, the stupid faculty who'd denied her the city she rightfully deserved, and she wouldn't look the other way either, at the classmates and crowd undoubtedly snig-gering at her failure.

She shook hands with the presenter, and while he pinned the tiny crossed-swords badge on her collar, her eyes betrayed her and slid towards the aud-ience. Her stomach flipped as she saw the crowd of parents and friends behind the rows of students, all the way to the back of the hall, twenty rows at least, illuminated by the late afternoon light streaming in through the ceiling-high windows to the right. Everyone had someone here to watch them graduate. Everyone except Weird Al—and her.

The presenter finished with her pin, muttered something to her, and offered his hand again. Mercury coldly ignored it and strode from the stage. It didn't matter. None of it mattered. Tumul Tuos was her city anyway, and no one could change that. She'd think of something. She'd take a day or two out, make some plans…

And she could always hope that Deviran would choose some other Overlording territory. He'd be stupid to, but then again, he was stupid, so. Mercury could hope.

All at once, mid-way down the steps off the stage, Mercury came to rigid attention, scanning the room. Somewhere out there in the crowd, an exchange of power had just taken place, and it felt… unusual.

But the final few students were backing up behind her and muttering, so Mercury headed back toward her seat, craning her head all the while and searching for some sign of whatever it was that had just discharged a dizzyingly quiet amount of power into the room.

She sat, and Sparky leaned over. "Okay?"

"Mm," said Mercury. "Did you feel…" She accidentally caught the eye of the student behind her and twisted back to face the front.

"Feel what?"

Mercury turned it over in her mind. It had felt like a large shot of power discharged very quietly—but perhaps it hadn't been. Perhaps it had only been a small discharge after all, something most people wouldn't have noticed.

But still, something about it had tugged on her. It very nearly felt like something she'd felt before, only she *knew* she'd never sensed that kind of discharge before.

She shook her head. "Never mind. Don't worry."

Sparky sighed and straightened. "It's fine, Mercury," she said, drily exasperated.

"I know you didn't win, but I promise, you'll live through it."

Mercury waved a hand for silence.

The power had just discharged again, and it had come from somewhere in the back corner, far away from the windows and light.

Impatiently, Mercury waited for the formalities to conclude. The crowd stood while the quartet played the exit march, and the stage party left, Mercury tapping her foot all the while.

The moment the last notes of the march died away, Mercury turned and headed to the back corner, weaving in and out of the students and parents who had seemed to explode slowly but inexorably out from the neat rows of seating, ignoring Sparky's calls behind her. Power, something that tugged in a way that was strange and familiar, all at once. She pushed her way through a family posing for pictures—and halted.

In the shadows of the back corner, Deviran stood with his family, with his stupid, smug little smile, looking as tall

and dark and stupidly alluring as ever.
Prat.

His mother, short but sleek, and his
father—tall, and utterly terrifying in a way
not at all diminished by his gleaming
smile—gushed over him, patting his back
and hugging him tight. Within moments
the Principal was there, glibly shaking
hands and congratulating them on the
success of their son. Something flickered
across his consciousness, and also Deviran's father's—some moment of recognition in response to what they were
saying.

But Mercury brushed it aside just as the
mother brushed melodramatic tears from
her cheeks and handed Deviran a silver-
wrapped package about as long as her
hand but half the width.

That. That was the source of the
strange, magical feeling. Mercury watched
hawk-eyed as Deviran unwrapped the gift.
A glimpse of gold set her pulse racing—
What was it? What did it do? Could she
steal it?—and then the paper fell away to
the floor, and Deviran stood staring

wordlessly at the object in his hands, and Mercury did too.

Wide-eyed, Deviran raised his gaze to his parents, and even from where she stood Mercury could hear the reverence in his voice as he thanked them.

But Mercury had eyes only for the object. No wonder she'd felt it discharge, and no wonder it had felt both strange and familiar. In Deviran's hands lay a glorious, sunshine-gold key, large and strong—and with a handle in the shape of a stylised fish, long, flowing fins curving to make the grip.

A Key. They'd given him a Key. And not just any Key, but *the* Key, *her* Key, the Artefact of Power belonging to *her* city.

A wordless noise of wanting rose in Mercury's throat. Who cared about being dux? She needed that Key.

Keep reading! Head to
http://www.amylaurens.com/books/kaditeos/castle
to buy your copy now!

ABOUT THE AUTHOR

AMY LAURENS is an Australian author of fantasy fiction for all ages. She doesn't usually write sad or horrific endings, but sometimes they just have to be done. Or, at least, they *were* done, whether or not they had to be. She's neutral good, after all.

In addition to moderately twisted little holiday stories, Amy has also written the portal-fantasy *Sanctuary* series about Edge, a 13-year-old girl forced to move to a small country town because of witness protection (the first book is *Where Shadows Rise*), the humorous fantasy *Kaditeos: Mercury* series following newly-graduated Evil Overlord Mercury as she attempts to acquire a castle, and a whole host of non-fiction.

INKLETS

Collect them all! Released on the 1st and 15th of each month.

INKLET #007
SEVENTY
LIANA BROOKS

INKLET #008
A Final Request for Mercy
AMY LAURENS

INKLET #009
the kitten psychologist
vs.
the kitten's owners
THEA VAN DIEPEN

INKLET #010
Answer the Question
AMY LAURENS

INKLET #011
Happily, Red
AMY LAURENS

INKLET #012
the kitten psychologist
tries to be patient
through email
THEA VAN DIEPEN

INKLET #013
DRAGON Tuesday
AMY LAURENS

INKLET #014
RED PLANET REFUGEES
LIANA BROOKS

INKLET #015
the kitten psychologist &
What The Kitten Did
THEA VAN DIEPEN

Cherry Blossom
AMY LAURENS

Alone
AMY LAURENS

the kitten psychologist
& The Kitten
Come To A Conclusion
THEA VAN DIEPEN

LEVEL NINE
LIANA BROOKS

To Dust
AMY LAURENS

Interchange
AMY LAURENS

Emalia's Lanterns
LIANA BROOKS

Dear Santa
AMY LAURENS

The Quilt-Maker's Scrap
AMY L. LAURENS